Merry Christmas Bcc

What a pleasure to be getting to know you!
Hope this story will encourage your family &
that Christmas will always be a wonder.

Sincerely,
Rolyn Brown

The Most Unlikely Night

Written by Robyn Brown

Illustrated by Debbie Apple

Dedication

To Morgan, Jordan, Evan and Keaton,

Your young lives brought angels to mind.
I'm so grateful God shines brightly
through each one of you.

Note: *The existence of angels is well documented in the Bible. The personalization of their characters and experiences is used here to highlight the amazing nature of God's plan in sending Jesus to earth as a human. It is in no way a statement of fact or dotrine about angels.*

Gabriel smiled quietly to himself.

Gabriel's Assignment

Gabriel smiled quietly to himself. He was considering the announcement he was about to make to the host of angels in heaven. The Son of God was going to be born a human baby on earth! He had known of this plan for ages and ages and now could hardly believe it was actually going to take place. Baby Jesus. It seemed such a contradiction to him. God in small form. The impossible becoming possible. God's specialty.

He woke himself back to reality and thought about his next meeting. The senior cadet angels would be the first to hear the news. These cadets were especially seasoned at helping him explain responsibilities to the less experienced junior cadets and plebs, who were new to the assignment of human relations. What a time to be new to the job of relating to humans! What a time, indeed. He had full trust in these senior cadets. Each was fully capable and their names reminded him of their talents and victories.

Alexandra, protector of mankind, was well known for bravely defending many people in perilous circumstances. The most famous feat had happened more than a thousand years ago when she had watched over baby Moses as he lay helplessly in a basket of reeds. Alexandra had kept the reptiles of the Nile at bay until Pharoah's daughter rescued the baby from the river.

Boaz, the swift and strong, had often been sent when the need was urgent and the angels of darkness were particularly threatening to God's chosen people. He had been assigned to Joshua's side during the conquest of the Promised Land. Countless battles had been won because Boaz fought on behalf of men.

Arielle, lion of God, had repeatedly shown fierce devotion in defending the Israelites from their enemies. When the king of Assyria with all his forces had encamped against the fortified city of Judah, it was Arielle whom God had sent to cut off all the mighty warriors who threatened His nation.

These amazing senior cadets were often sent to help and serve men and women in all kinds of critical circumstances. Gabriel had confidence in his officers. He knew they would make sure the heavenly society of angels accomplished all they were commanded on behalf of God's people.

Alexandra, Boaz and Arielle arrived and drew close to Gabriel, their eyes full of expectation and loyalty.

"It's time," Gabriel said simply. "The long awaited moment is here. We must alert the junior cadets and plebs. They need to understand their role in all that will take place these next few months. It is imperative that we shine our brightest at this moment in the history of mankind. The Holy One has invested everything in this plan to save His humans. They need us now more than ever."

Alexandra spoke first. "Gabriel, we are ready to serve. It is an honor to be chosen."

"Yes, we are ready," Boaz added confidently. "Nothing will stop our mission."

Arielle spoke in earnest, "The junior cadets and plebs will be our first priority. We will help them understand."

Gabriel nodded. "You are strong of heart. I know you will serve well. Remember to be patient with the other cadets. They are faithful like you, but the plan is still new to them. Remember how you felt when you were first told? Give them room to embrace the idea. They will eventually understand as we have."

The senior cadets left to announce the angel gathering. Gabriel readied himself, straightened the sash on his uniform and thought back over the details of the strategy he was about to convey. He was so privileged to be the one to make the announcement. This was very good news!

It's Time!

Living in God's presence produced a perpetual joy among the heavenly beings, but today they were particularly energetic with anticipation. Gabriel spoke with authority to call them to order. "Your attention please angels! Angels, please...your attention!" As he raised his hand, Gabriel gazed out over a sea of upturned faces, now quiet, waiting for him to continue.

"This is a momentous occasion, unparalleled in the entire universe. It is both our privilege and challenge to be part of the Father's plan for mankind and it is my great honor to make this announcement." Gabriel paused, overwhelmed again at the significance of what he was about to say and then finished solemnly. "It is time."

The noise began again, softly, and then intensified. Angels in small groups exchanged awestruck glances and launched into enthusiastic jabber. Gabriel's look of serious wonder broke into a smile as he overheard the group of junior cadets nearest him remarking to one another.

"It's time!" exclaimed Mari.

"It's time!" repeated Alpha.

"Oh boy, it's time!" shouted Zion.

"It's time for what?" asked Doron quizzically.

"It's time for the Son to go to earth," explained Arielle, who recognized her first opportunity to help this group of junior cadets. "We have all been waiting for this for many years."

"It's for the Son to go to earth," explained Arielle.

"I know, it seems like an eternity," said Zion jokingly, knowing full well that it had been an eternity since the birth of this plan. His smile melted into seriousness as he realized that his name, Zion, meant 'a sign' and he wondered what role he would play in what was about to happen.

"It's hard to believe he's finally making the journey," Mari pondered. She was more awestruck than the others that this long awaited event could actually be happening and it would soon be clear to her why she felt that way. Mari meant 'wished for child'.

Gabriel pulled his attention away from the amusing conversation and called the assembly to order once again. "It is time for the Son of the Holy One to go to earth," he continued. "This truly is an extraordinary event and we will all be involved. We must make preparations."

An eager voice came from the middle of the gathering,. "Should I pack his royal robe for him?"

"Will he need his golden sash?" another offered helpfully.

"No," Gabriel answered. "He won't need his robe or his sash. He won't be taking anything."

"What will he wear?" asked Doron. The junior cadet whose name meant 'gift' did not understand the plan that everyone else seemed to know so much about.

"He won't be wearing anything at first," responded Boaz. He was prepared for the gasps he heard from the plebs that had gathered around him to hear Gabriel's announcement. Shana, Gurit, and Zephan all had special assignments in the coming months but they would never have guessed the details that they were about to hear.

"Will that be alright?" whispered Shana, looking expectantly at Boaz for an answer.

"He won't be wearing anything because he's going to earth as a baby," Boaz explained gently, trying to calm the young angel's misgivings. She was so tenderhearted and aptly named 'God is gracious'.

Now a chorus of surprised comments came from the far side of the assembly.

"A BABY!", exclaimed one.

"A baby?", said another in disbelief.

"Are you SURE?" questioned a timid voice from the front.

"How can that be?" questioned Gurit, the next newest angel cadet in the group whose name meant 'innocent baby'.

"How's he going to fit inside a baby?" inquired Doron, now feeling more bold since there were others who did not seem to understand either. Even a junior cadet sometimes needed clarification. The angel beside Doron turned to Arielle and asked doubtfully, "Do you think that will work?"

"How could that possibly work?" interjected Zion.

Gurit had been quietly reasoning and now added, "Maybe he's going to be a very large baby."

"No," responded Boaz. "He's just going to be the standard size."

"I don't know," said Zephan. Though not the youngest cadet, Zephan, which means 'treasured by God', was still in preliminary training and quite dumbfounded at what was being

"Are you SURE?"
questioned a timid voice from the front.

proposed. "I just never pictured the Exalted One as a helpless little human."

"I can hardly picture it at all," agreed Gurit, hoping someone would explain the paradox.

Gabriel held up his hand almost apologetically. "I know it sounds impossible," he admitted, "but remember the Father can do anything."

"That's true," asserted Alexandra. "He can do ANYTHING! Besides, this is the way He wants it to be."

"Yes," Gabriel continued. "He has wanted it this way from the very beginning."

A hush fell over the myriad of angels as they contemplated what Gabriel was telling them. A plan of God, older than themselves coming to fruition before their very eyes. Extraordinary! Yet it all seemed so unlikely.

An exclamation broke the silence as an angel, overcome with wonder yelled, "It's quite an amazing plan, don't you think!"

"Revolutionary!" decreed another.

"Still," Alpha interjected, "it does seem unlikely that the Creator would want to become a baby." The junior cadets agreed but were interrupted in thought when the plebs, carried away by the idea of a baby, began voicing their excitement.

"I love babies." proclaimed Shana.

"They're so soft!", added Gurit. "How did God make them so soft?"

"Babies are cute!" joined another.

"They're sweet too," said a third.

"Babies are cuddly," stated a fourth. "I'm so glad they're cuddly," another agreed.

Shana again spoke up, "He'll have little toes," and held up a thumb and index finger close together to demonstrate the size.

"And little fingers," chimed Gurit who held up both hands in excitement.

"He'll have little toes."

"A little mouth and nose, too," added Zephan. Everyone was beginning to envision a sweet, tiny human baby and the impossibility of the idea was starting to fade.

Gurit breathed deeply and said, "Babies smell nice."

"Ugh, sometimes they don't," came back a response.

"Yes, but he'll make sweet noises," said Gurit undaunted.

"I love the little noises," nodded Shana in agreement.

Zion spoke up as though puzzled, "I wonder if He'll like it inside that tiny body?" The plan was not new to Zion but now he was beginning to think of it from the Son's point of view.

"I don't think he'll like it in there a bit," declared Alpha and then added as if to explain the statement, "He won't be able to do anything himself." Even this junior cadet, whose name meant 'firstborn' had to voice her questions.

"What a change that will be for him," Mari said thoughtfully. "If he can't take care of himself, who will take care of him?"

Arielle joined in now, "Yes, if he's going to be a baby he will need someone to take care of him."

The new cadets began to bubble again. "I will," announced Zephan with gusto!

"I will," declared Shana.

"Me too," joined Gurit.

"Me three," shouted Doron.

"We all will," pronounced Zion. The enthusiasm of the young cadets was contagious even for a more experienced angel.

"Do you think we could?" Shana asked hopefully as she looked up at Alexandra. "I definitely think we could do a great job!"

Alexandra put her arm around Shana's shoulders and replied, "No, Shana, the Father already has everything arranged. He's chosen some very special humans for the job."

"Humans," gasped Gurit. "Are you sure?"

Doron stepped forward in earnest and asked, "Will they take good care of the Prince?"

Arielle reassured them. "The Father trusts them to take care of His Only Son."

"Wow, THAT is a lot of trust" agreed Zion, who was becoming more amazed at each new detail he heard.

"Who are the lucky people?" inquired Zephan.

The group became quiet waiting for the answer to that very important question. "You know them," offered Alexandra, "Mary from the town of Nazareth. And her fiance, Joseph."

"Oh, I bet they'll be so surprised," chuckled Zephan, eyes dancing with enjoyment.

"They'll be surprised alright," agreed Doron.

Boaz projected to the whole group as if to dismiss the meeting. "Remember, The Exalted One has been planning it this way for a long time. Gabriel has just left to begin the arrangements."

Zechariah's Answer

abriel had witnessed the Lord do some amazing things before but this idea made even parting the Red Sea seem insignificant. He still hardly believed it! He was accustomed to living where the splendor and majesty of the Creator filled every nook and cranny. Heaven was a place that glowed with the presence of The Holy One. He was everywhere and in everything. To imagine a limit on His being or power in any way seemed so unlikely.

His surprise over God's plan was only surpassed by his astonishment over God's method of revealing the plan! Gabriel had thought so many times about what it would be like to announce the arrival of the Son of God. He had envisioned a gigantic, worldwide assembly! Every person on earth, great and small, young and old, wise and foolish would gather with excitement to hear a royal proclamation from God Himself. The trumpets would blow the regal entrance song, the crowd would hush with anticipation and God's voice would resound with the glorious news. And when they heard that the Holy Prince was going to live among them teaching and healing, they would all be so thrilled! They would overflow with gratitude and excitement and shower the new prince with precious gifts and praise that would bring a smile to the Father's face lasting into eternity.

But that was not the plan. Not at all. No assembly. No trumpets. No royal proclamation to the masses. No fanfare. Gabriel's list of people to tell beforehand was really quite short. Four people. Imagine the Son of God visiting earth and only four people alerted beforehand!

Gabriel was still stunned at this surprising method, but being experienced at watching the Father's plans unfold, he was certain about two things. Somehow this was THE best plan and somehow it would all work out PERFECTLY. There was absolutely no question in his mind about that. The challenge before him would be to convince the humans involved to have the same confidence. Sometimes, just as he encountered Daniel many years ago, he found men humble and eager, responding with understanding and insight. At other times he had interacted with men who had greater difficulty embracing heavenly ideas. He wondered what he would find today.

This assignment was to alert the parents of the prophet to be born just before Jesus. John would be Jesus' cousin and would prophesy to the people about the coming Messiah. The father and mother of a prophet had to be carefully chosen. They simply had to be devout, faithful people.

In swift flight he arrived at his destination, the temple in Jerusalem, to find worshippers assembled and praying outside. He positioned himself inside the temple beside the altar of incense. Zechariah, the recipient of his message today, was

"Zechariah, God has been listening to your prayers all these years."

fulfilling his duty to burn incense. He shuffled along, old as he was, toward the altar and when he saw Gabriel he froze with fear. Somewhat accustomed to this response from humans, Gabriel was quick to reassure him.

"Zechariah, you don't have to be afraid. I'm here because God has been listening to your prayers all these years. He heard every one. You and Elizabeth have wanted a son for a long time and NOW you're going to get what you prayed for! About this time next year, Elizabeth will have a baby and you'll name him John and he will be the joy of your heart. What's more, he is going to become so godly that even the Holy One will consider him a great man."

Zechariah was trying to digest all that was being said to him, but Gabriel hadn't finished speaking.

"Since John will be set apart for such a divine task, he is never to have wine to drink," stated Gabriel. "He is going to be a prophet for God so he will have the Holy Spirit inside him from the minute he is born. You see, Zechariah, your son John is going to play a vital role in the salvation of everyone on earth because he's going to preach to the people and help their hearts be ready to believe in Jesus. He'll be so powerful he will remind you of Elijah."

Gabriel gazed intently at Zechariah, eager to hear his response. "So what do you think, Zechariah? Isn't this thrilling news?"

Gabriel could see that his message was not having its desired effect. In fact what happened next was unthinkable! Zechariah doubted that Gabriel was telling him the truth! "How can I know this will happen?" Zechariah questioned. "I'm practically as old as dirt and my wife is really old and it's impossible for people as old as we are to have children."

Now Gabriel was indignant. This message was meant to be a blessing received with joy! The answer to years of earnest prayer. Gabriel would have thought old Zechariah would muster his strength and do a back flip but here he was responding with faithlessness. How dare this man, priestly family or not, question God's plan! He stood his straightest, set his jaw, and lowered his voice. "I am Gabriel," he declared. "I stand in the presence of God, and HE sent me to you to tell you this good news. What I have told you WILL come true and because you did not believe my words, you are not going to be able to talk at all until all these things take place." Zechariah opened his mouth to apologize for being ungrateful and faithless, after all this really was incredibly great news, but no words came out. Not even a peep.

Gabriel vanished as quickly as he'd appeared, leaving Zechariah holding his silent throat, wishing he could have a second chance at a more appropriate response. It took him quite a while to gather his wits. What had just happened? He'd only heard of angels, never seen one. And this news. He was going to be a father? The father of the prophet of God's coming messiah? It was surprising and seemed altogether unlikely.

While this unfortunate scene was occurring in the temple, the worshippers outside had begun to talk among themselves.

"Hey do you know who is on incense burning duty today?" asked a man named Jacob.

His neighbor responded, "This month the priests of Abijah's division are here. When they drew lots, Zechariah was chosen, so I guess the old guy finally got his turn."

A third man joined in, "What do you think could be taking him so long?"

19

"Well, you know Zechariah. He is so faithful and righteous. And his wife Elizabeth is such a faithful, devout woman. Maybe he's in there praying extra," offered Hadassah, who had overheard their conversation.

"Could be," said Jacob, "or maybe he can't find the incense!" The three men chuckled thinking about the possibility.

"Well, I sure hope he comes out of there soon. I've got to get home," Hadassah added. "I have a lamb in the oven."

Just then Zechariah came out of the temple and tried without success to explain what had happened inside. Since he couldn't speak he kept making signs with his hands.

"What happened, Zechariah?" asked Jacob. "What are you saying?"

"He's not saying anything," said Hadassah. "I think he saw something."

After awhile they stopped trying to understand him and left without knowing anything at all about the amazing plan that Gabriel had just revealed to Zechariah. For the moment this special announcement from God would still be kept very quiet.

Zechariah stayed at the temple for the rest of his two week time of service then went home to the hill country of Judea. Unlikely as it was, old Elizabeth became pregnant and praised God for blessing her with a child. Zechariah didn't have anything to say about the impossible thing that was happening before his eyes, but he was thinking a lot. He was thinking God could make about anything He wanted to out of dirt!

Mary's Faith

*I*t had been half a year since Gabriel had spoken with Zechariah at the temple in Jerusalem and his indignation had worn off. He shivered as he contemplated again the next set of events on the verge of unfolding. Now it was time to reveal the plan to the people chosen to be the parents of the Christ. He wondered how his message would be received. Certainly no person had ever heard anything like this before!

Nazareth was a city in Galilee, a small community of families that until now had no particular significance. It was there he went to find Mary, fiancee of Joseph and future mother of Jesus. Without difficulty, he found her family's home and watched Mary for a moment before he spoke. She was a young adult, and though not unusual in appearance, he knew her to be a woman of unusual devotion to God, faithful and full of integrity. By the faraway look on her face and the happy tune she was humming he wondered if she was picturing her upcoming marriage to the man of her dreams, Joseph.

"I am God's servant.
Let all you have said come true."

His appearance startled her so he spoke up, hoping to calm her fears. "Hello Mary," he said. "Your heavenly Father is so pleased with you and He is with you."

The uncertainty in her heart was obvious on her puzzled face. Who was this man, how did he know her and what was he saying to her?

"Don't be afraid, Mary," Gabriel continued. "God is so impressed with you! He has chosen you out of all the women in Israel to be the mother of His child. You will give birth to a son and name him Jesus. He will be great and will be called the Son of the Most High. The Lord God will make him a king like his ancestor David. He will be the king of Israel forever and his kingdom will never end." He paused, hoping her faith would allow her to avoid Zechariah's plight of silence. He did not want to have to get tough with this very nice young lady. He was relieved to be able to sense her acceptance of what he told her even before she spoke. In fact she accepted it so quickly that she immediately asked a question about how it would happen.

"How will this be," she asked him, "since I am a virgin?"

He began his explanation. "God's power and His Holy Spirit will create a baby within you so that the child to be born will be called holy - the Son of the Most High." Gabriel had to admit that even he did not understand this in all its complexity nor did he have a further explanation than what he had already given so he quickly proceeded to the next part of his news.

"God is doing another miracle right now through your very old relatives who everyone thought would never have a child. He has made Zechariah and Elizabeth parents! They are going to have a baby. In fact she has been pregnant for six months. You know nothing is impossible with God!"

Gabriel finished and looked expectantly at Mary, waiting for her reply. Again, she came through with flying colors! She not only believed his message, but gladly embraced it. She spoke deliberately and humbly, "I am God's servant. Let all you have said come true."

Now it was Gabriel's turn to be surprised. This truly WAS an impressive young lady. Faithful and humble in a circumstance that had never been heard of on earth. Gabriel left her, praising God for His choice of this godly young woman to be the mother of Jesus.

Joseph's Dream

A short time later, Joseph, the man of Mary's dreams had a dream himself. He was tossing and turning as he tried to go to sleep. His mind was full of restless doubts, disappointed hopes and conflicting desires. What had happened? His beautiful bride-to-be had completely stunned him with the news of Gabriel's visit. No matter how many times he replayed their conversation in his mind he had not been able to find a way out of this impossible situation.

"Joseph," Mary had said, "I need to talk to you. Something very amazing and exciting happened today and I want to tell you all about it! Maybe you should sit down. Here, please sit right here and I'll tell you what happened."

What's so important, he'd thought to himself. Probably some new development with the wedding he had guessed. "It's a good thing we're just doing this wedding thing once," he'd muttered under his breath as he sat in the chair beside Mary. He had silently finished his thought, 'I don't think I can take much more of this!'

"An angel visited me today," she had said as she took his hand in hers. He had barely been able to keep quiet while she told him of the plan Gabriel had revealed that she would be the mother of God's only Son. At her first pause, he had jumped up from his chair and said, "Look Mary, if you don't want to get married, you can just say so. You don't have to invent some wild story to scare me away!" He continued indignantly, "If you have done something shameful you need to be honest and tell me the truth."

She was hurt but still tried to explain. "Joseph, you are the man of my dreams. Please trust me. I need so much for you to believe that I am telling you the truth. I would not make this up. I know it's hard to imagine but I really need your trust right now."

"Mary," he'd said, "how can you possibly expect me to believe what you are saying? I have never heard anything so absurd in my life." He kept imagining the look he had seen in her eyes. She seemed so hurt. She really expected him to buy this story! Well, that was just too much. He knew he wasn't the smartest guy around but he was no fool either. He was smart enough to know a lie when he heard it!

He had barely thought of anything else since that day. Her interaction with Gabriel was so hard to believe and yet she believed it without question. To see and speak with an angel was unlikely enough, not to mention being told this inconceivable tale. The Son of God, born to his fiancee! He wanted to trust her integrity but her story was just too bizarre. She couldn't be telling the truth. There must be something she was hiding.

Engagement was a binding agreement and when it became known that she was pregnant before they were married, the disgrace would ruin both their families. He had decided to solve this embarrassing situation by ending their engagement

"Mary," he'd said,
"how can you possibly expect me
to believe what you are saying?"

quietly. He was hurt and heartbroken but he was not vindictive. He did not want to see her publicly humiliated.

As he fell into a deep sleep an angel appeared to him in his dream. Boaz, who had been looking forward to helping Joseph understand this incredible circumstance now spoke as gently as he could. "Joseph, son of David, do not be afraid to take Mary as your wife. The baby inside her really is from God. She is telling you the truth. She will give birth to a son and you will name him Jesus, because he will save his people from their sins."

Joseph woke up and shook his head in disbelief. "Was that an angel I just heard?" he said out loud. "You're kidding! Was that guy for real? I think he was!" then his voice trailed off as he realized he was talking to himself. He got up and paced for a few minutes and then the idea started to settle in. Mary had been telling the truth! What a relief and yet what an amazing situation this was! Isaiah had prophesied that the virgin would be with child and would give birth to a son that would be called Immanuel, which meant 'God with us'. How did he get picked to be the father? Well, not really the father. If God was the father of Mary's baby, what did that make him?

"I think it makes me the guy who had better do what this angel character is talking about!" he blurted, this time not caring that there was no one to hear him.

Joseph took Mary home to be his wife and out of reverence for the Lord, he waited to become one with her until after the baby was born. His determination to heed the angel's message proved that, once again, God had chosen wisely the humans that were to take care of His son.

"The baby inside her really is from God."

Praising God

Mary's decision to travel south to the hill country of Judah to visit Zechariah and Elizabeth had been made in great excitement. Joseph had told her of his dream, the angel's confirmation of the news she had received from Gabriel, and his decision to go through with their marriage even under such exceptional circumstances. Now she was free to enjoy the blessing of her position and Elizabeth's long awaited answer to prayer. She shared a special connection with Elizabeth even though they were decades apart in age. Both of them filled with child, both children specially anointed by the Holy Spirit.

She entered the house where her relatives lived and greeted Elizabeth with great affection. At her words, Elizabeth felt her baby leap within her and the Holy Spirit filled her and she exclaimed loudly, "Mary, you are a blessed young lady! Among all the women I know, you are the most blessed. And the baby inside you is blessed as well. Why am I so fortunate to have the mother of my Lord come and visit me? When I heard your

"My soul is full of admiration for the Lord and I am rejoicing in God my Savior."

greeting, the baby in my womb leaped for joy. Mary, you are blessed because you believed that God would do what He said and make you the mother of His only son."

Mary was filled with wonder and appreciation to God at these kind, encouraging, spectacular words from Elizabeth. Now it was her turn to express her praise to God.

"My soul is full of admiration for the Lord and I am rejoicing in God my Savior. He has looked down on me, even though I am no one special, and has seen that I am His servant. From now on everyone who hears about me will know that I am a blessed woman because God has done this great thing through me and He is holy! He is merciful to anyone who fears Him no matter what generation they live in. He is showing Himself to be so powerful and strong. No matter how much the prideful puff themselves up God makes them as though they are nothing. People who are humble in heart, He lifts up. People who are hungry, He feeds. People who come before God thinking they have all they need are turned away without receiving anything. Because of His mercy He has remembered His promise to Abraham to bless the entire world through him."

The days and months ahead were filled with many conversations between Mary and Elizabeth about visits from angels and the sons they would soon nurse. They hoped Zechariah's voice would come back so he could share in their joy.

Elizabeth's delivery of a baby boy brought her relatives and neighbors to her home to rejoice in the mercy that God had shown her. When the baby was eight days old his parents brought him to be circumcised, according to their custom and as an expression of thanks to God for His blessing. Those gathered for the occasion asked Elizabeth what name should be given to her son, and fully expected her to answer, "Zechariah, after his father." They were all startled when she answered, "No, his name is John." This reply brought confused looks and questions, "But why? No one in your family has that name?" They looked to Zechariah and waited patiently for him to finish writing his thoughts. This was a process they had become accustomed to these last months. He held up the tablet so they could see what he had written - 'His name is John.'

Immediately after he finished writing the name Zechariah was able to speak again. He had been wondering for months if his voice would really come back and when it did he decided his first words would be praise for God. The Holy Spirit filled him and he shouted, "Praise the Lord God of Israel! We are His people and He has come to visit us. He has shown His great strength by making a way for us to be saved through the family of David, His servant. Just as all the prophets of long ago predicted, He has come to save us from our enemies. He remembers what He promised Abraham, to care for us and save us so that we can serve Him righteously all our lives without being afraid of anything."

Zechariah picked up his new son and said, "And you, my little son, will be called the prophet of the Most High. You are going to teach the people to get ready to see their Savior. You will teach them about salvation and the forgiveness of sins. Our God is so merciful. His son will be a light for all the people who don't know the Father. He will teach us how to live in peace."

All the neighbors who had gathered there were frightened. They had never seen or heard such things. Nevertheless, they spread the word quickly through all the towns in the hills of Judea. People couldn't stop talking about Zechariah and his encounter with Gabriel or the miracle of Elizabeth having a son in her old age. Everyone wondered if their new baby boy would grow up as Zechariah predicted and be the prophet of the one who was

"His name is John!"

35

going to save them all. No person among them could have imagined what was yet to come.

Mary, filled with wonder, returned to Nazareth and waited prayerfully for the day when her child would be born.

Bethlehem

*R*iding a donkey to Bethlehem was not Mary's preferred activity so late in her pregnancy. Family history, which sometimes seemed so distant and unrelated, came fully into view as they plodded along.

Elimelech, whose ancestors were the Ephrathites, had lived in Bethlehem ages ago before a famine forced him to move to the land of Moab. His son married Ruth, whose ancestors were the Moabites and she had proven to be a woman of conviction, character and faith. Ruth had journeyed back to Bethlehem after both she and her mother-in-law lost their husbands. Then she met and married Boaz. Their son Obed had a son named Jesse, who had eight sons, the youngest of whom was David. Imagine a king in her husband's lineage! Unfortunately the benefits of being related to royalty were not very obvious at the moment.

Caesar Augustus had decreed that everyone in the world should go to the town of their ancestors and be registered. Joseph's family had ancestry and a rich history in Bethlehem, so off they went, all the way from Galilee to Judea. Somehow the journey seemed longer to Mary than when she had come that way a few months ago to visit Elizabeth! As they went on their long and tiring, 70 mile journey, they imagined the relief they would feel when they reached Bethlehem, found a place to stay and got to rest for awhile.

Finally they arrived but the relief they were looking forward to was not to be found. Every inn was full and overflowing with the abundant descendants of David who had come to register because of a whim of the Roman Emperor! Or so it seemed.

"Mary, I know you are exhausted," Joseph said sympathetically. "This is not at all what I wanted for you and our son, staying in a stable with no real bed for you to rest. I am so very sorry."

Mary reached reassuringly for Joseph's arm. He had been heroic and very attentive to her these last months. All she wanted now was to rest quietly and soothe away the ache she felt in her lower back. This baby would come soon and she knew that just as the entire pregnancy had been miraculous, God would be watching over the birth. She was tired but she was at peace. God had been only faithful to them and she knew that wasn't going to change.

A Quiet Entrance

The Son of God came quietly into the world, among animals in a stable. Wrapped in cloths and laid in a manger where livestock ate. His young mother and her husband witnessed his birth, amazed that the prophesied Savior would make his entrance into the world in such unlikely circumstances.

Not Such a Boring Job

The young men watching over a flock of sheep on a hillside near Bethlehem were unprepared for the excitement that was ahead of them on what was otherwise an ordinary night.

"There isn't a lot of glory in this job, is there?" Ari asked rhetorically. He didn't really expect his five comrades to answer.

Yered decided to answer anyway. "No," he said, "but somebody has to do it."

Zakai thought of a joke and added quickly, "Makes me feel kind of sheepish." That brought clods of dirt whistling in his direction, even though the darkness prevented good accuracy.

"It's dark tonight," pointed out Uri, noting that none of the dirt clods hit their target.

"Yeah, here we are again, watching these dumb sheep out here in the dark," moaned Seth. Being the youngest in his family he had little hope of ever being promoted past sheep duty.

Baruch now spoke up, "This job is getting so boring. It seems like nothing exciting ever happens out here. Are you guys bored? I sure am. I think the sheep even look bored tonight!"

"Yeah, yeah Baruch, we're all bored. And since there's nothing we can do about it, maybe you should just pipe down!" scolded Uri who had little tolerance for complaints.

Yered the most sensible of the group added, "Hey, better bored than scared. I'm just glad the lions don't seem to have noticed us. We don't need that kind of excitement."

"Speaking of lions, did you guys hear that?" Zakai whispered nervously, pointing toward the nearby hillside. "I think I saw something!"

Ari was quick to retort in his firmest voice, "Knock it off Zakai, you're scaring Seth. There is nothing to be afraid of anyway. You know that."

At that moment the sky lit up. An indescribably bright light shone all around them. Each shepherd raised his arms across his face as a shield from the brilliance. As they grew accustomed to the light they lowered their arms and fear gripped their hearts as they saw the angel, hovering in the sky above.

Alexandra had been eager for this moment to declare God's long awaited news and spoke with zeal, "Don't be afraid. The good news I am bringing to you will be joyful for all the people everywhere! Today in the city of Bethlehem the Savior has been born, who is Christ the Lord. And this is how you will

know who he is. You will find a baby wrapped in swaddling cloths and lying in a manger."

Instantly as she spoke, a huge number of angels also appeared. The shepherds would never know them by name, but the junior cadets and plebs didn't mind that at all. Mari, Alpha, Zion and Doron all knew they had a special role in proclaiming this news to the young men before them. Shana, Gurit and Zephan had been anxiously awaiting this moment as well. Now they all raised their voices along with countless other angels and praised God saying, "Glory to God in the highest, and on earth peace among those with whom He is pleased!"

Then as quickly as they had appeared, the angels left them and ascended back into heaven. The shepherds were all stunned

and looked wide-eyed at one another, unsure if what they had witnessed was real.

"Wow, who were those people?" asked Seth. "And where did they go?"

Uri answered confidently, "Those were angels, Seth, straight from heaven. Pretty amazing, that's for sure!"

"Maybe this job isn't as boring as I thought!" remarked Baruch.

As it dawned on them that what they had seen WAS real, they began to erupt with excitement.

"Let's go to Bethlehem and look for this baby!" they said to one another. Then without another thought about their tired, boring sheep, they quickly made their way to Bethlehem.

Finding Joseph and Mary and the baby just as the angel had said only intensified their wonder. A baby, in a manger? And here he was. After they admired him for a little while they began boldly proclaiming to anyone who would listen all that they had seen and heard from the angel that night.

Just as Gabriel had encountered different reactions to this message, the shepherds found a variety of responses to their message. The people in that area wondered what they were hearing and what was going to happen. Some believed, some didn't and some didn't even care.

Mary kept these things in her heart and thought about them as would any mother of a newborn son.

The shepherds went back to their fields but now their hearts were full of praise for God and they glorified Him for all that they had seen and heard.

"This baby will become a light for the Gentiles and a glory for your people Israel."

Aged Blessings

The time came for them to go through the purification ceremony written in the Law of Moses, so Joseph and Mary took Jesus to Jerusalem to present him to the Lord. Since he was their firstborn son and holy to the Lord, they sacrificed two young pigeons at the temple.

Simeon, an old, old man was led by the Spirit to come into the temple while they were there. He was a righteous and devout man and God had revealed to him that he would not die before he saw the Lord's Christ. He took Jesus in his arms, knowing full well that when he peered at this tiny face he was looking at the Savior of the world. He blessed God and said, "Lord, now you are letting your servant die in peace, just as you promised me for now my eyes have seen your salvation that you have been planning. This baby will become a light for the Gentiles and a glory for your people Israel."

Then Simeon blessed Joseph and Mary as well. "Your son has been appointed by the Almighty to be the salvation of everyone, but not everyone will obey him. Some people will believe him and find their way to God, but others will oppose him. His coming will expose what is in the hearts of many people."

The young couple was amazed at all that this godly man was saying to them about their son.

An old widow named Anna was there also, giving thanks to the Lord and speaking about Jesus to everyone who had been waiting for the arrival of the Savior of Israel.

Following the Star

After Jesus' birth wise men from the East came to Jerusalem asking about the child that had been born king of the Jews.

"We saw his star," they explained, "and we have come to worship him." When Herod the king heard of the wise men and their quest he became greatly troubled. Many people in Jerusalem were troubled at the news of an infant king. Herod assembled the chief priests and scribes of the people to ask them where the Christ was to be born.

The answer was clear. "In Bethlehem of Judea," they said. "The prophet Micah wrote that Bethlehem, in the land of Judah, will not be just an insignificant town; for out of her will come a ruler who will shepherd God's people."

So Herod called the wise men secretly and found out the exact time they had seen the star. He sent them on their way to

Bethlehem instructing them to make a careful search for Jesus so that he too might go to worship him.

Leaving Herod, they followed the star they had seen in the East and were overjoyed to see it stop over the place where they would find the child. By that time he was no longer a newborn and Joseph had found a house to stay in while they waited to go back to their home in Nazareth. Finding Mary inside the house with Jesus they bowed down and worshiped him. Opening their treasures they presented him with gifts of gold and incense and myrrh. Somehow these visitors from a foreign land seemed to understand more than most what they were witnessing and in whose presence they had been privileged to come.

Once again God used a dream to give his instruction to men. They were warned not to return to Herod's palace to tell him they had found Jesus. Instead they returned to their land by another route. As they traveled they rejoiced and praised God that He had chosen them to see the king He had sent to earth.

"We saw his star," they explained, "and we have come to worship him."

Gabriel's Reflections

Gabriel stared off at the stars. Heaven had seemed a little quiet lately. There had been so many preparations to make and now, in the blink of an eye, the big event had happened. Jesus had been born on earth. He still couldn't quite take it in. God had become a human baby who would go through all the pains of growing up like every other child. He would get hungry and thirsty and cry to be fed. He would fall down and skin his knees as he learned to walk. He would learn to talk by practicing and learn to do every day human things like reading and making furniture. He would go to the temple with his parents and sit and listen to men describe how God took care of Israel. Gabriel wondered if Jesus would remember how he himself had created the earth with his Father long ago or if it would all be new to him as a human. Such strange questions came from this amazing plan.

There didn't seem to be any answers to his questions so Gabriel resigned himself to waiting. He and all of heaven would wait patiently while God's baby son grew up to be a man. They would watch him eagerly, as God would, and find delight in every part of his life. The pleasure on God's face was obvious to all the angels. His son was growing up and would imitate his Father. How fitting.

The great event might be over but Gabriel still thought about it often. He remembered the fear and wonder he had seen in the people who had witnessed it. They were few in number, but their account of that unprecedented blessing to all mankind, would echo through the ages. He knew that as with all things pertaining to the Almighty, human and angel minds alike, had struggled and would always struggle to grasp the endless power and holiness of God's workings and plan. Amazing, awesome, brilliant, incredible and to some...most unlikely!

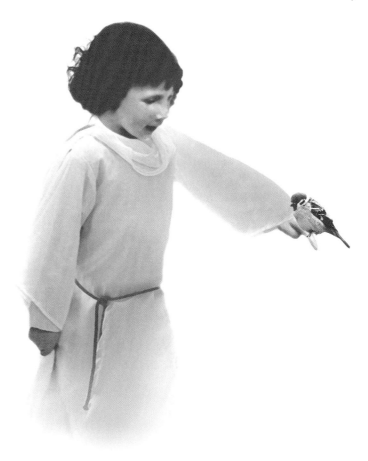

Bible Characters

(Non-fictional Characters)
Found in the account of Jesus' birth in the Bible:
Matthew 1:18-2:12 and Luke 1:5-2:40

Gabriel (God is my strength)
archangel, recorded in the Bible to have been
God's messenger to Daniel and Mary

Zechariah (Jehovah has remembered)

Mary (beloved)

Joseph (He will multiply)

Elizabeth (promise of God)

Simeon (listening)

Anna (gracious)

Herod (song of the hero)

Chief Priests
religious leaders of the Jewish people

Scribes
professional students and interpreters of the Law of Moses

Wise Men
priests from Persia - tradition records three kings,
although the Bible does not mention their royalty or number

The Angels and Shepherds

(Fictional Characters)

<u>Senior Cadet Angels</u>

Alexandra (protector of mankind)

Arielle (lion of God)

Boaz (swift and strong)

<u>Junior Cadet Angels</u>

Alpha (firstborn)

Doron (gift)

Mari (wished for child)

Zion (a sign)

<u>Plebs (New Cadets)</u>

Gurit (innocent baby)

Shana (God is gracious)

Zephan (treasured by God)

<u>Worshippers</u>

Jacob (to follow, to succeed)

Hadassah (myrtle tree)

<u>Shepherd Boys</u>

Ari (lion)

Baruch (blessed)

Seth (appointed one)

Uri (light)

Yered (to come down)

Zakai (one who is pure)